Counting

Illustrated by Colin Twinn

1 One

Can you find
Susan's crown?

Today's the day of the summer fair;
Susan is Queen of the May.

2 Two

How many swings
can you see?

Next Susan and William have a ride on
the swings. Father is keeping an eye on
Tom and Harry.

3 Three

How many
ice cream
cones?

How many
are pink?

What a hot day! Mother buys everyone
an ice cream cone – even baby Victoria.

4 Four

How many wheelbarrows
in the race?

Oh dear, Tom has fallen out.
Polly thinks a skipping rope is safer.

5 Five

How many
coconuts
are there?

Look! Susan has hit a coconut with her first throw.

6 Six

○ ○○○ ○ ○

Can you
count the hoops?

Who is going to win the race?
Come on Polly, Susan's in front.

7 Seven

How many cakes
can you see?

It's time for a delicious cake.
William likes pink ones best.

8 Eight

How many
ribbons
can you
count?

Mother is leading the maypole dance.
The bunnies like dancing.

9 Nine

How
many
balloons
are
there?

Whose balloon will go furthest? William
can write his own name on his label.

10 Ten

Can you
count
all the
cups?

Who is going to break the most cups?
Naughty Tom thinks he can cheat.

How many coconuts can you find in the picture?

How many teddies?

The fair is over and it's time to go home. They've had a lovely day, and look at all their prizes!

FREDERICK WARNE

Published by the Penguin Group
27 Wrights Lane, London W8 5TZ, England
Viking Penguin Inc., 40 West 23rd Street, New York, New York 10010, USA
Penguin Books Australia Ltd, Ringwood, Victoria, Australia
Penguin Books Canada Ltd, 2801 John Street, Markham, Ontario, Canada L3R 1B4
Penguin Books (NZ) Ltd, 182–190 Wairau Road, Auckland 10, New Zealand

Penguin Books Ltd, Registered Offices: Harmondsworth, Middlesex, England

First published 1988
3 5 7 9 10 8 6 4 2

ISBN 0 7232 3564 3

Printed and bound in Great Britain by
William Clowes Limited, Beccles and London